THE DOG
WHO BELONGED TO NO ONE

By AMY HEST   *Illustrated by* AMY BATES

Abrams Books for Young Readers, New York

The illustrations in this book
were created using pencil and watercolor.

Library of Congress Cataloging-in-Publication Data

Hest, Amy.
The dog who belonged to no one / by Amy Hest.
p. cm.
Summary: The hard-working daughter of two bakers and
a perfectly nice stray dog live lonely lives in the same town,
until they meet one very stormy day.
ISBN-13: 978-0-8109-9483-6 (hardcover)
[1. Loneliness—Fiction. 2. Dogs—Fiction.] I. Title.
PZ7.H4375Dnm 2008
[E]—dc22
2007012763

Book design by Chad W. Beckerman

Printed and bound in China
10 9 8 7 6 5 4 3 2 1

HNA ▪▪▪▪▪
harry n. abrams, inc.
a subsidiary of La Martinière Groupe
115 West 18th Street
New York, NY 10011
www.hnabooks.com

For Kate and Billy,
who belong to each other.
—A.H.

For Alex, for everything.
—A.B.

ONCE there was a small dog with crooked ears. He belonged to no one.

And once there was a wisp of a girl named Lia.

The dog who belonged to no one was a perfectly nice fellow, with a perfectly nice temperament. He was not a loud barker. Nor was he a biter, jumper, fussy eater . . . or grumbler.

Lia lived with her mother (a baker) and her father (a baker) in a crooked little house on the edge of town. It always smelled wonderful there, like bread in the oven . . . and cake. The porch had a soft night light.

The dog who belonged to no one tried hard to be helpful every day. When the baseballs of summer sailed into the woods, he found the baseballs. When the air turned cold and mittens went missing, he found the mittens. Not that anyone took notice of a small dog with crooked ears.

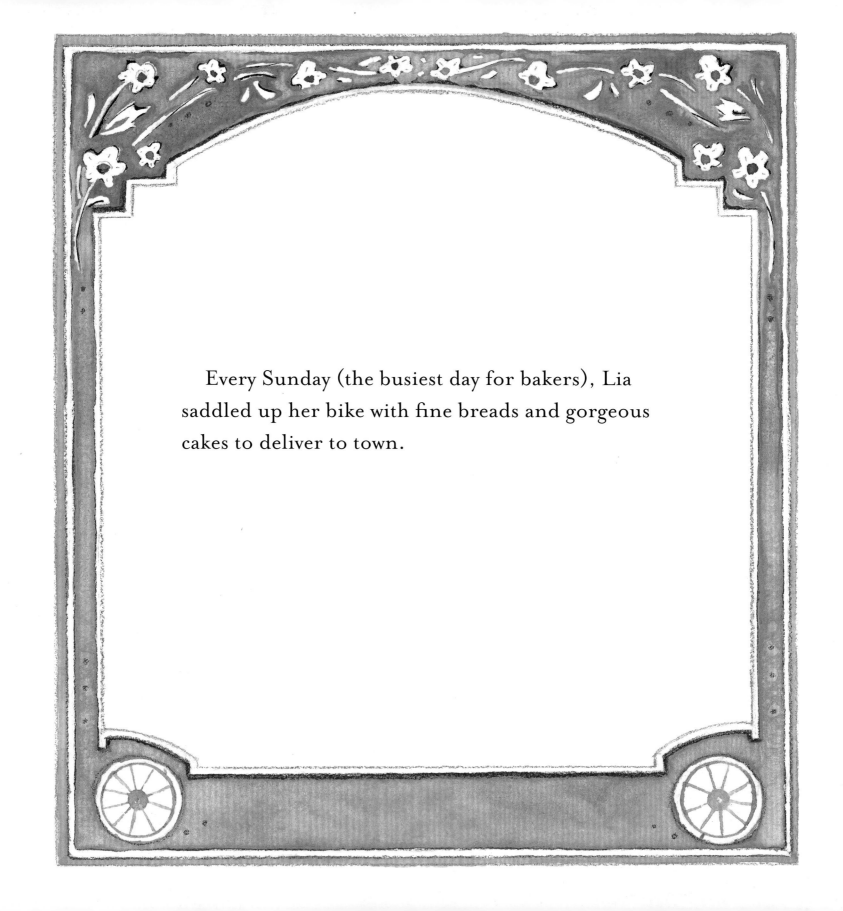

Every Sunday (the busiest day for bakers), Lia saddled up her bike with fine breads and gorgeous cakes to deliver to town.

The dog who belonged to no one spent his days quite alone, exploring the narrow streets and wide boulevards of town after town . . . all through the changing seasons. He longed for a friend.

There were many high hills . . . and Lia pedaled very hard. Her legs grew tired. To make herself feel less alone, she thought up stories as she pedaled. The stories were like friends on her long ride to town.

As day turned slowly to night, the dog who belonged to no one tried to outrun the night . . . run, run, run . . . but a small dog could not outrun the night.

As the dark grew darker, he trembled. He shook. To make himself less lonely, he pictured a yard and a porch with a soft light. He pictured a cozy corner, where he could tuck himself inside himself and dream of belonging to someone.

And as day turned slowly to night, Lia pedaled all the way
home . . . pedal, pedal, pedal . . . to the crooked little house,

where she climbed into bed and tucked herself inside herself
and dreamed.

One Sunday morning, a storm whipped into town, a great big Sunday soaker. The dog who belonged to no one tried to outrun the storm. Run, run, run!

At that very moment, on that very Sunday, a wisp of a girl was racing home. Pedal, pedal, pedal!

But the small dog could not outrun the storm.
How wet he was. Soaked to the bone.

Lia was soaked. Right to the bone.

He shook. He shivered. He dripped. When the wind blew, his crooked ears blew.

She shook. She shivered. She dripped. When the wind blew, her hair blew, too.

The dog who belonged to no one ran and ran to the
edge of town and onto the porch of the crooked little house.
Lia pedaled and pedaled to the edge of town, right to the porch,
where her parents were waiting, and a small dog was waiting, and
the soft light was on.